NO
ELEPHANTS
ALLOWED

For Justin and Stefan

Houghton Mifflin/Clarion Books
52 Vanderbilt Avenue, New York, NY 10017

Printed in the United States of America

Library of Congress Cataloging in Publication Data

Robison, Deborah.   No elephants allowed.
Summary: Justin must think of a way to get rid of the elephants that
bother him in his room each night.
[1. Night —Fiction] I. Title.
PZ7.R56538No   [E]   80-21404   ISBN 0-395-30078-9

NO ELEPHANTS ALLOWED

BY DEBORAH ROBISON

 Houghton Mifflin/Clarion Books/New York

Justin knew that every night
after he got into bed
an elephant came into his room.

Everyone said it wasn't true.

"It's impossible, Justin," said his sister.
"There's no elephant near here."

"Don't worry, Justin," his father said.
"An elephant can't come in our house."

"It isn't real, Justin," said his mother.
"It's only a dream."

But Justin knew that every night
an elephant came into his room.

And not only one.

Sometimes two.

One day Justin's father came home with a present
for Justin. It was a toy rabbit.
"This rabbit will help you with those elephant problems,"
said Justin's father. "He will sleep next to you
and be your friend."

The rabbit was soft and fuzzy,
and Justin liked to hold him at night.

But the rabbit didn't keep the elephants away.

"I have a good idea," said Justin's mother.
"Let's build you a new bed. A place just for you.
No elephants allowed."
So Justin and his mother sawed and hammered
and painted—and they made Justin a new bed.

It was a cozy bed and a
strong one. Justin liked
to sleep there with his rabbit.

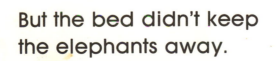

But the bed didn't keep
the elephants away.

It didn't keep the lions away, either.

"Look Justin," his sister said.
"This is a special light for you.
I'll put it in your room and
you can turn it on yourself.
Now you can SEE that there are
no elephants or lions here."

Justin liked his new light.
When he was in bed with his rabbit the light could make
the darkness disappear from the corners of his room.

But the elephants and the lions were still there.

And they brought the alligators with them.

Just before bedtime one night, Justin was
sitting in the living room looking at magazines.
The magazines were full of pictures and
Justin loved pictures.

He turned one page and then another page.
And then he saw a picture that made him smile.

"Mother," he said. "I need the scissors.
I want to cut out a picture to hang up in my room."

"How nice," said his mother. "A pretty picture in
your room will make you feel better at night."

Justin took the magazine
and scissors to his room
and closed the door.

"A picture of flowers
would be good," his father
called. "Are you cutting
out flowers?"

"No," answered Justin.

"Did you find a clown?"
his sister asked. "A clown
could cheer you up."

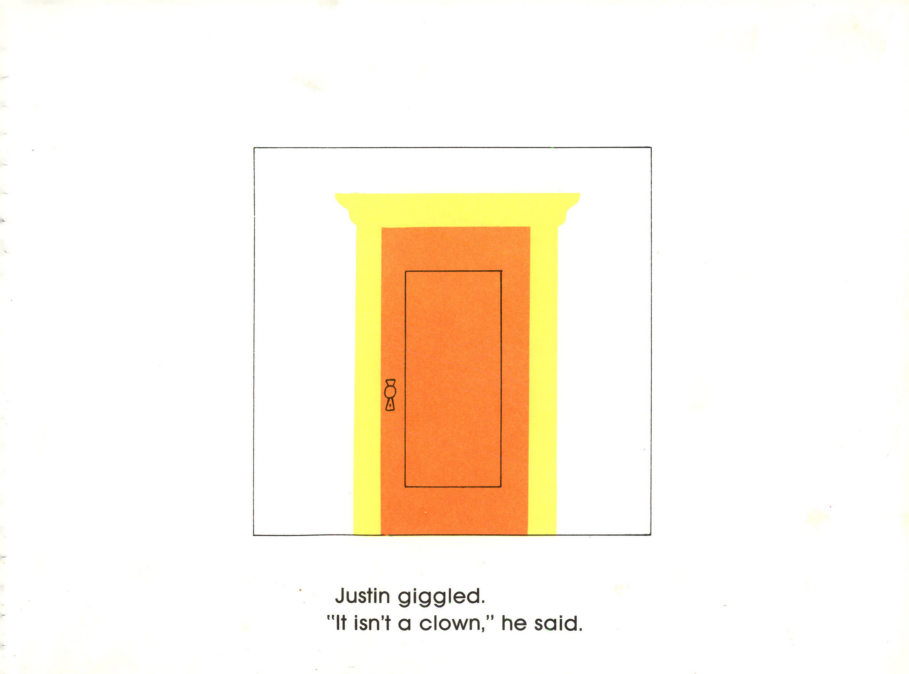

Justin giggled.
"It isn't a clown," he said.

Finally Justin opened his door.
"I'm done!" he said. "Look!
That's my picture."

"Now I have a gorilla to protect me!"

Justin climbed into bed and went to sleep.

And the elephants, the lions, and the alligators never came back again.

DATE DUE	BORROWER'S NAME	ROOM NO.
9/21/04	Izabella	2